Chubby Little Stubby to the Rescue

Afton Nursery School
Chase your dreams
BP.

BETH PYSNACK

Illustrated by Frances Espanol

To order additional copies of this book, contact:
Xlibris
1-888-795-4274
www.Xlibris.com
Orders@Xlibris.com

ISBN: Softcover   978-1-7960-5467-5
         EBook   978-1-7960-5466-8

Print information available on the last page

Rev. date: 08/22/2019

Chubby Little Stubby to the Rescue

There once was a chubby little corgi named Stubby. Stubby had a very important job that he did with his mom. He was a search and rescue dog. Stubby found people who were lost in the woods.

Chubby Little Stubby wasn't a very fast dog, for he had very little legs. He wasn't a very agile dog, as he was aptly named "Chubby" Little Stubby.

This didn't stop Stubby though, for his skill lie within his nose.

His little black nose would twitch, and it would turn. It would wiggle and it would waggle and would tip back and forth until it pointed his stout little body in the direction of people smells.

One sunny morning, Chubby Little Stubby was on a mission to find a lost little boy in the woods.

The little boy had wandered away from his campsite while chasing a hop toad. He was alone and scared, but remembered his mommy saying if he didn't know where to go, it was best to stay where he was.

The little boy cried for his mommy and was getting hungry, so he nestled deep inside the trunk of a tree to stay warm with his new pet hop toad he had named Herbert.

That morning Chubby Little Stubby geared up for the job. His mom put on his search vest with his favorite jingle bell so she could hear him going through the woods.

Stubby cast his stout little nose to the air and he was off to find the little boy and bring him home to his mommy and daddy.

The deeper Stubby got into the woods, his little nose began to twitch and turn. It began to wiggle and waggle. It tipped back and forth until it pointed into a thick patch of trees. Chubby Little Stubby gave a "yip" and followed his nose to a hollowed-out tree.

He first encountered a frightened little toad clutched in two ice cold hands.

"That's Herbert," a soft, shaky voice whispered. "What's your name?"

Chubby Little Stubby knew this had to be the little boy he was looking for. He gave the boy a warm, loving lick across the face to comfort him. Stubby then told the boy to stay where he was. "I'll be right back," he told him. "I have to tell my mom where you are."

Stubby then took off as fast as his little legs could carry him. His jingle bell chimed its sweet tune to alert his mom that he was on his way back to tell her something.

"Bark, bark, bark," Stubby said. Which translates roughly to "I found him mom, come with me."

Stubby's mom gave him the cue "show me" as Stubby spun around like a top spinner and barreled his way back through the weeds to the frightened little boy.

Stubby jumped through the opening of the tree into the boy's lap, being careful not to squish Herbert. He curled around the boy's waist while licking his hands and soothing his sores from the pricker bushes. Stubby's mom reached in with a soft, warm blanket, cradling them as she lifted them from the tree trunk. Stubby was tired after searching all day and extremely happy that he was helping bring the boy home. He drifted off to sleep in the boy's lap. Comforted by Stubby's soft, warm fur, the boy too, drifted off as they emerged from the woods in the arms of Stubby's mom.

The boy's mom could barely contain herself at seeing her son safely delivered home. She gently took him from the embrace and cradled him close to her chest. She softly whispered in the boy's ear how much she loved him and how glad she was that Chubby Little Stubby had brought him back to her.

The boy's mom began to walk away with him in her arms, thanking Stubby the whole way. As she moved away, a soft voice came from her snuggled little package with a simple request:

"Can I keep Herbert?"

CPSIA information can be obtained
at www.ICGtesting.com
Printed in the USA
BVHW020804080919
557820BV00003B/11/P